Trapped In Waku Waku Romance

Alice Beauverd

Published by The naughty witch's bookshelf, 2023.

This is a work of fiction. Similarities to real people, places, or events are entirely coincidental.

TRAPPED IN WAKU WAKU ROMANCE

First edition. November 27, 2023.

Copyright © 2023 Alice Beauverd.

ISBN: 979-8231992553

Written by Alice Beauverd.

INTRODUCTION

The evening light trickled through the curtains, casting shadows across Yuki's room. It was alive with color from posters of Waku Waku Romance is favorite Japanese dating sim games, stacks of books, manga and games surrounding him everywhere - everything he loved crammed together in his small sanctuary. Yuki sat hunched forward at his computer desk, his fingers flying over the keyboard while soft melodies drifted out of speakers into the cozy, chaotic room. In his world, nothing else mattered except the characters and stories that lived inside these screens. Every time he felt lonely or stressed, he would immerse himself further into those digital landscapes, where he could explore endless possibilities of love and friendship—a place far more enticing than reality itself.

Tonight, however, something strange happened. Yuki was so consumed in his fantasy world that he didn't notice the whispering voices growing louder until they filled his ears entirely.

"What do you wish for?" The voice spoke suddenly and clearly. Without moving from his chair, Yuki replied without hesitation, "To live inside my favorite game, Waku Waku Romance." he said while clenching the game's box. "Granted," the disembodied voice answered, filling the silence left behind. There was no flash of light or sudden change. One moment, Yuki was alone in his dimly lit room, and then...nothing. Confused but excited, Yuki stood up slowly from his chair, stretching after being seated for hours. His hands moved instinctively towards his body, feeling reassured upon finding familiar sensations intact – despite having just wished to exist inside another universe. This must all be some kind of illusion or dream, he thought uneasily. But if it were true...he might finally get what he always wanted! Yuki couldn't help smiling wryly at the idea. If only this weren't a dream or simulation, he mused, thinking about how amazing it would feel to step foot in Waku Waku Romance, interacting with the game's heroines directly rather than merely observing through a screen. He start imagining having sex with each of them in explicit detail, visualizing every act, position used during sex. Feeling turned on, he started getting aroused as each mental image escalated his sexual desire. Each scene played out in vivid detail in his imagination, his hand unconsciously rubbing against his own crotch, trying to quell the throbbing erection forming there. The sights of the curvaceous, pixel-perfect bodies danced around in his head as his breath grew faster and heavier. With a deep sigh, he surrendered fully to his impulses, reaching down underneath his jeans, pulling out his hardened member with trembling hands. Gripping it tightly, Yuki pictured one of the women from the game, a deliciously busty brunette named Ami. Her plump lips parted slightly, anticipation building within her eyes. Her breasts rose and fell with heavy breaths, subtle movements that made Yuki's heart race even harder. Taking hold of his penis firmly, he began to stroke its length, gradually increasing speed, allowing the tip to glide effortlessly along the tender skin of his palm. As he increased pressure, pleasure built rapidly, sending jolts throughout his whole body. It wasn't long before his excitement reached a boiling point. Overwhelmed with ecstasy, he thrust backward onto his chair, moaning involuntarily. The sounds of his orgasm echoed faintly amidst the quiet of his room. Unable to contain the wave of relief flooding his body, Yuki let loose, splattering his stained sheets with hot liquid as his seed spurted forth. Exhausted yet elated, he collapsed onto his pillow, breathing heavily. Even though he had taken care of his physical needs, a lingering sense of emptiness remained. Reality seemed distant now; perhaps too much distance existed between him and the rest of humanity. After such intense moments, Yuki couldn't help but feel a bit empty afterwards. Spend, he lay there, staring blankly at the ceiling, he slowly fall asleep, exhausted physically and mentally. However, he seems to hear whispers again. "now, what to do?" They seem concerned, unsure. "What even is this Waku Waku Romance ? I think he want to be the character on the cover right? That girl?" she asked uncertainly, glancing towards the poster of the game on the wall. "let's just do it" Another disembodied voice chimed in, sounding somewhat weary. Soon after, Yuki lost consciousness.

WAKING UP IN WAKU WAKU ROMANCE

As the sun peeked through the slats of the blinds covering the window, a gentle warmth caressed Yuki's cheeks. Curling beneath the covers, he found himself relishing the silky smooth texture of the sheets. Despite the pleasant atmosphere, a nagging sense of unease crept upon him. Something felt different. Uncomfortably so. What's going on here? he wondered, scrambling to sit upright. Opening his eyes, the first thing he saw wasn't the usual mess of clothes and scattered game's case lying near his bed. Instead, he found himself surrounded by vibrant colors, lace patterns, and a cute decor befitting a teenage girl's room. He notice long pink hair cascading downwards. Looking down, he see large, perky breasts protruded gracefully from underneath a cute pink pajama top which barely concealed them. His gaze continued downwards,encountering rounded hips and legs encased in matching bottoms. These curves seemed quite foreign to him, causing confusion mixed with curiosity. startled, he leapt off the bed. Scanning the area quickly, he stumbled upon an ornate piece of furniture that caught his attention. It was a vanity table, adorned with intricate carvings. As he approached it cautiously, he noticed amirror mounted above the surface of the table. Intrigued by what he might see reflected in the glass, he raised himself up on tiptoes and peered into the polished surface. What greeted him there left him utterly speechless and filled with dread. His once unremarkable facial features had undergone a startling transformation. Yuki now beheld two pink eyes staring back at him, wide and apprehensive. The reflection before him was undeniably feminine. Realization struck like a thunderbolt. Yuki was not in his room anymore, nor was he inhabiting his body.No, he had been magically transported into the world of Waku Waku Romance, like he wish for. But instead of being Hiro, the male protagonist, he had become Momoko, the game's main heroine.

Terrified by the uncertainty of his predicament, Yuki frantically searched his surroundings, seeking answers.

What...what happened?" His new high pitched voice quivered ever so slightly. He swallowed nervously, looking down at his feminine frame, struggling to accept this unexpected metamorphosis. Was he still dreaming? No, he realized with horror, the changes to his appearance confirmed otherwise. This had actually happened; he really was in Waku Waku Romance, albeit in the form of its titular heroine, Momoko. Murmuring under his breath, Yuki muttered curses and profanities, unable to comprehend why his harmless wish had resulted in such an extreme consequence. All he desired was a temporary escape from reality, indulge in virtual fantasies of romantic interludes with beautiful game avatars. Little did he know that this innocent desire would manifest so literally and catastrophically. Now, as he looked down at his own chest, his breasts seemed to mock him in return.

He tried shifting his weight from one leg to another, attempting to adjust to the sudden difference in bodily proportions. His attempts proved futile as he fidgeted helplessly, desperate to regain control over his circumstances.

The once comfortable confines of his own home felt incredibly remote now. How could things have gone so horribly wrong? His face clouded with anger and self-pity, he glared fiercely into the mirror. As tears threatened to well up in his eyes, he couldn't help but remember the countless hours spent playing Waku Waku Romance. Never in his wildest imagination did he think he'd find himself within its confines - especially as the curvaceous heroine he admired most. Glancing around the room, he recalled every detail about how these surroundings appeared in the game. Each item, no matter how insignificant, took him further away from reality. However, despite the shock and disbelief coursing through his veins, an odd excitement seeped in. Perhaps this bizarre turn of events might provide some amusement after all? Contemplating this idea brought a slight smile to Yuki's lips.

"So I guess this is my new body," he murmured, examining his reflections carefully. With a deep sigh, he admitted defeat. "Might as well make the best out of this situation." He thought, running his fingers across the lavish fabrics lining the canopy of his bed. "After all, if I've gotta live in Momoko's shoes, I may as well enjoy myself!" He then plop on the bed, feeling its softness embracing him. He ran his hands along the pillows, smelling the delicate scents emanating from them. Taking in the sight of his surroundings, he grinned mischievously. After all, why should he limit himself to merely experiencing life as Momoko? Why not also experience it with more explicit pleasure? Thought Yuki, his heart throbbing faster with anticipation. He stretched , allowing his body to acclimate itself to its newly acquired femininity. Leaning forward slowly, Yuki began exploring the new terrain of his bosom. Cupping his palms around the firm yet supple flesh, he closed his eyes and savored the sensation.

He then proceeded to undo the buttons that adorned the top of his pajamas.

Allowing it to fall open, exposing her ample cleavage. He glanced into the mirror again. His hands traced the contours of his breasts, sending thrilling sensations

coursing throughout his body. Experimentally, he pinched his nipples, eliciting a rush of intense arousal. His erect nipples stood proudly, achingly sensitive to even the lightest touch. As he rubbed his thumb across their puckered tips, waves of exquisite pleasure coursed through his body.

He start feeling his new body respond sexually. His pussy grew wetter, moistening the fabric between his legs. Feeling increasingly excited, he let his hand explore the rest of his body.

Yuki cupped his breast tenderly, massaging it gently. A wave of electric energy shot through his core, making his pulse race.

As his hand drifted lower, he pressed his fingers against the edge of his panties, dipping into the damp folds that hid treasures beyond imagining. Slipping a finger in between those sweet petals, he encountered velvet softness, slick with desire. Moisture clung onto his digits, drawing them deeper into his depths. Reveling in the pleasing resistance, Yuki curved his index finger inward, pressing against something that sent shivers through his spine.

Enjoying the tantalizing sensation, he pushed harder, creating an intensity that sent spirals of ecstasy surging through his body. With each gentle push and pull, Yuki's need only intensified. Soon enough, he couldn't resist reaching down to stroke his swollen nub, applying just the right amount of pressure to send jolts of pure delight crashing through him. Yuki bit his lip, holding back a whimper as he slipped his middle finger alongside his index, pushing deeper than ever before. His mind raced with images of Hiro's face as he pushed closer to orgasm.

He began thrusting his fingers rhythmically in time with his rapid heartbeat, building momentum. His mouth watered, tongue swirling erotically around his teeth. His mind played tricks on him – visualizing Momoko entwined in passion with Hiro. But instead of imagining himself as Hiro, like he usually did during solo play sessions, he was Momoko. As he imagine being swept into passionate moments shared between the two avatar counterparts, his cheeks blushed crimson with embarrassment. His finger slid in and out of his hot cavern, quickening the pace as his heart raced. His breath came in ragged gasps, echoing through the silent room. As his body trembled violently, he reached down, grasping his throbbing clit, pressing hard until his whole body convulsed. Closing his eyes tightly, he threw his head back, letting out a shrill cry. Shudders wracked his body while he climaxed, muscles tensing and relaxing with the force of each contraction. Breathlessly, he collapsed onto the bed, overcome with satisfaction.

Now that he had discovered the power of his newfound sexual prowess, Yuki decided to test the limits of his ability. Gazing into the mirror once more, he allowed his fingers to trail teasingly over the curve of his hips and up the length of his thighs. He caressed his silky skin, reveling in the sensual feel beneath his fingers. Unable to suppress his curiosity any longer, he leaned forward to gaze upon the fullness of his breast. It didn't take long for his fingers to trace the pathways downwards, finding the warmth between his legs. Sliding his hand inside his panties, he found the welcoming warmth waiting for him there. The moistness made him eager for more intimate contact. Curiosity piqued, he hesitated briefly before deciding to taste his own sweet nectar. He parted his lips invitingly, bringing his finger to his mouth. Drawing it close, he touched his tongue to the tip, savoring the salty tang mixed with his essence. The contrast between the sweet and savory flavors ignited a fire within him, making his entire body tremble with anticipation. He stroked his fingers against the sides of his throbbing nub, coaxing forth a moan of pleasure that reverberated in the quiet room.

Unbidden, a vision flashed through his mind: Hiro bent over Momoko, taking her roughly from behind. Overwhelmed by the desire to experience that very scenario firsthand, causing a stirring sensation low in his belly. Envisioning himself as Momoko beneath Hiro, his breath caught as he imagined their bodies moving together in perfect sync. As his thoughts wandered, his body followed suit, writhing beneath him as his hips rolled seductively. Arching his back, Yuki knew exactly what he wanted. His fingers roamed higher towards his firm breasts, kneading them lovingly. As they brushed against his budding nipples, he closed his eyes, relishing the sensation. They were ripe, standing tall under his touch, begging for attention. Desire flowed through him like a river, guiding his movements instinctively.

Reaching toward his chest, he tweaked one of his pert breasts, causing a tide of wantonly pleasure to cascade through him. Grasping at his other breast, he subjected it to similar treatment, driving him mad with desire. Squeezing his engorged nipples, he moaned in ecstasy, lost in the heightened sensitivity of his body. As he continued to explore his new form, unabashed desire consumed him. Allowing his fingers to dance across his aching clitoris, he experienced an explosion of blissful release unlike anything he could have ever imagined. Convulsing in the aftermath of powerful pleasure, Yuki lay there, dazed and exhausted. His entire body felt numb, as though every fiber was still resonating with the aftershocks of his climactic journey.

Gradually, the weight of fatigue settled upon him, and he pulled himself off the bed, wandering aimlessly through the confines of Momoko's chamber. Unaccustomed to his curves, his limbs seemed heavier, but the strangeness only served to fuel his fascination with his new figure.

He paused midway through adjusting his clothes, struck by a sudden epiphany. His transformation wasn't merely physical—it start to affect his mental state too! Intrigued by his newfound femininity, Yuki decided to further explore these altered feelings. Standing before the mirror, he admired how the sunlight danced across his curvaceous figure. Each line added to his frame accentuated his womanhood, making him appear more and more attractive. As he watched, he noticed a sense of vulnerability emerge in Momoko's demeanor. This vulnerability intrigued him, reminding him of a secret he held dear within his own heart. This connection brought comfort to his spirit - despite feeling somewhat alienated in the foreign landscape of his new body. Taking another moment to appreciate his appearance, he marveled at the subtle grace of his movement.

Turning away from the mirror, he surveyed the contents of Momoko's room, familiar to him thanks to his extensive hours spent playing the game. Despite his initial unease with his changed form, his fascination with his surroundings continued to grow. The delicate lacework on the curtains cast an air of romanticism throughout the space. Glancing towards the nearby windows, he saw the reflection of trees rustling outside, bathed in golden afternoon sunlight. He realized with a start that if he looked closely enough, he might catch sight of some cherry blossoms amidst the verdant greenery.

Realizing he hadn't eaten all day, Yuki rummaged through Momoko's kitchen cupboards for sustenance. Upon discovering some fresh fruit nestled among canned goods, he smiled. Nibbling on a slice of apple, he observed the room around him. Realizing the necessity of self-care even in such fantastical circumstances, he ventured to the bathroom. As he entered, he noted the luxurious array of products lining the vanity. A variety of lotions, soaps, and perfumes filled shelves, awaiting use. Steam rose from the bathtub, creating a misty veil that obscured the edges of the room. Feeling emboldened by his recent exploration of Momoko's body, Yuki stripped, allowing the heat to seep into his pores. He took in deep breaths, filling his nostrils with the scents of the steamy atmosphere. He began by taking a shower, allowing the warm water to cascade down his body, cleansing him of lingering traces of his prior activities. As the steaming water coursed over his sensitive flesh, the exquisite pleasure it invoked caused goosebumps to rise along his arms and neck. Brushing his hands through the trickling stream, he let the rippling currents dance over his exposed body. He couldn't help but notice the way his wet skin gleamed under the light streaming through the window. With each stroke of his fingertip, he reveled in the texture of his now feminine body. The sensation sent thrills down his spine. Yuki couldn't believe just how responsive his new body was. He ran his hands through his hair, tracing the contours of his head, feeling his silken locks slip through his fingers. The sensation was indescribably pleasurable. Yuki's fingers moved rhythmically across his erect nipples, eliciting responses far beyond simple arousal. Their tips swelled further, growing increasingly tender, responding to the gentle pressure applied. The feeling intensified with each passing second, building steadily to a crescendo.

As he rubbed the delicate flesh between his thumb and index finger, the sensation grew stronger and stranger than anything he'd experienced before. Throbbing with excitement, he pressed harder, reveling in the sharp pain intermingling with sheer delight. He use the shower's head to massage his erogenous zones, slathering himself in the soap suds, which clung seductively to his newly sensitive skin. The cool droplets from the falling water raked teasing paths down his quivering body, tantalizing him with each caress. The sound of the water drummed against the tile, providing an entrancing backdrop for his musings. His fingers traced their way lower, seeking out the warmth hidden beneath his folds. He grasped his moist entrance with steady determination, slipping two well-lubricated digits inside him. Delight radiated from the base

of his spine, shooting upward in waves of pure euphoria. Yuki pushed deeper, reveling in the exhilarating friction. Every thrust produced a satisfying groan that echoed within the confines of the steamy bathroom. The pleasure reached a fever pitch, culminating in a surging orgasm that left him weak-kneed and breathless. For several moments, he remained motionless, reveling in the afterglow. Gradually, his racing pulse slowed, replaced by the thumping of his rapidly returning circulation.

He turned off the shower, letting the water drain away, leaving behind a trail of puddles on the tiled floor. He then entered the bathtub, slowly lowering himself into the warm, soothing water that enveloped him. As the hot liquid encased him completely, he found himself drifting into a peaceful meditation. His mind returned to his former existence, where he had been a shut-in who lived vicariously through video games.

Having spent an adequate amount of time soaking in the warm water, he finally decided that it was time to exit the tub. Standing carefully, he grabbed a fluffy white towel hung near the edge of the tub, wrapping it snugly around his body to cover his modesty.

Emerging from the steamy bathroom, he made his way back to Momoko's bedchamber.

Clad in his pajama set, Yuki sat on the edge of the bed, staring blankly into space. Lost in thought, he absentmindedly fingered the collar of his nightwear. Stifling a yawn, he stretched out on the bed. Curling onto his side, Yuki buried his face in the pillow, drawing in the sweet fragrances lingering within the fabric. Gradually, exhaustion crept upon him. Soon, he drifted into a dreamless sleep.

MEETING HIRO

The morning sun filtered through the curtains, casting soft rays that illuminated the room in a subdued glow. Yuki woke, groggy from last night's adventures. Rising from the comfortable bed, he walked over to the dresser to get dressed.

Reaching toward the drawer where he assumed his undergarments would be kept, Yuki hesitated briefly. Still, curiosity got the better of him, and he opted to give it a try. After donning a pair of lacy panties and bra, Yuki took a moment to examine himself in the full-length mirror affixed to the wall. Adjusting the cups of the bra ever so slightly, he stepped back to observe his image. Satisfied with what he saw, Yuki picked up Momoko's school uniform from the closet and put it on. The fitted skirt hugged his legs tightly, accentuating his shapely calves. Meanwhile, the blazer fit snuggly around his shoulders, highlighting the contour of his chest. As he buttoned the buttons one by one, he couldn't help but take note of how his bosom protruded ever so slightly beneath the fabric.

The doorbell rang, causing Yuki to jolt upright. "It must be Hiro," he thought, recalling the game's events. Opening the front door cautiously, Yuki tried hard to conceal his nervousness while maintaining composure. As Hiro approached, his eyes lit up when he recognized Yuki in Momoko's attire. "Hello, Momoko! You look lovely today." Yuki couldn't help but feel a wave of embarrassment rush through him, accompanied by a hint of pleasure at receiving compliments. Unable to speak for a few seconds due to his anxiety, Yuki merely nodded and gave a faint smile in response. Swallowing hard, he attempted to engage in conversation, hoping to ease the awkward silence between them. "Thank you, Hiro." Yuki felt his cheeks redden as he spoke, still struggling to control his nerves. Hiro grinned warmly, his voice resonating with genuine admiration. "Of course, Momoko. You look very charming in your uniform." Hearing those words only served to increase Yuki's discomfort, amplifying the flush spreading across his face. Yet, despite his obvious insecurities, there was also something undeniably exciting about the attention. He could feel his heartbeat quicken as Hiro gazed appreciatively at him. This wasn't supposed to happen. It shouldn't have happened like this - Yuki mentally berated himself. But standing here, wearing Momoko's uniform and experiencing these intense feelings, Yuki couldn't deny the truth of the situation. Overwhelmed by conflicting emotions, he struggled to maintain eye contact with Hiro.

" So, Momoko, do you want to accompany me to school?" asked Hiro earnestly.

In all honesty, he hadn't considered attending school alongside Hiro as Momoko. Besides, he reasoned, if he were truly going to play the role of Momoko effectively, he needed to immerse himself fully in her reality. Taking a deep breath, Yuki replied decisively, "Yes, let's go to school together, Hiro." There was no turning back now. Embracing the unfamiliar sensations flooding his body, Yuki strode towards the exit. putting on his shoes, he followed Hiro outside. As they made their way to school, Yuki couldn't help but feel incredibly self-conscious in Momoko's clothes. His skirt brushed against his bare leg, sending shivers down his spine. His hands trembled slightly as he adjusted the hem, ensuring that nothing showed below the length.

As they continued walking towards school, Hiro couldn't resist stealing glances at Momoko's well-endowed figure swaying gracefully beside him.

In his head, he imagined wrapping his arms around her slender waist, pulling her close, feeling the gentle curves of her body pressing against his own. Hiro swore to himself that tonight, after classes had ended, he would make his move. However, before anything else could transpire, they arrived at the entrance of the prestigious Sakura High School. With a mix of excitement and trepidation, Hiro led Momoko inside.

As she navigated the hallways adorned with elegant murals depicting ancient folklore, Yuki found himself growing increasingly aware of his outfit. Each step caused the pleats of his skirt to rustle lightly, eliciting fleeting looks from curious students. Unaccustomed to such heightened scrutiny, Yuki felt vulnerable and exposed, yet strangely thrilled by the attention. His heart thumped rapidly, echoing his rapid breaths. As he walked through the crowded hallways, he couldn't help but notice the way some of the male students' gazes seemed fixated upon his chest. In particular, a group of three boys who appeared to be talking amongst themselves suddenly turned their heads simultaneously, ogling at Momoko with rapt expressions. Feeling unnerved, Yuki hurried along the corridor, attempting to lose himself amidst the sea of other students.

Hiro noticed Momoko 's apprehension and sought to reassure her. Putting his arm protectively around her shoulder, he said, "Don't worry, Momoko. I won't let anyone harm you." Yuki blushed deeply at Hiro's gesture and was grateful for his support. Deep down, however, he couldn't help but wonder about his changing feelings towards Hiro. Was this just another side effect of becoming Momoko? Yuki couldn't stop thinking about his newfound feelings. The fact that he was aroused by Hiro disturbed him, considering he had never been interested in men before. Perhaps it was because of his current appearance – Momoko's femininity coupled with the influence of the game? Or maybe this was a manifestation of his true desires, buried deep within him? Regardless of the cause, Yuki couldn't ignore the palpitations in his chest every time he looked at Hiro.

As classmates gradually filed into the classroom, Hiro remained seated beside Momoko, occasionally shooting covert glances at her curvaceous form nestled demurely behind the textbook. Though Yuki grew anxious from the persistent stares directed towards his ample assets, he maintained his focus on studying alongside Hiro.

Later that day, during lunch break, the two sat together near the cherry tree-lined courtyard. As they shared a quiet conversation while nibbling on bento boxes, Hiro observed Momoko surreptitiously from the corner of his eye. Her delicate fingers caressed the handle of her chopsticks, and her lips moved subtly, lost in her thoughts.

Across from her, Hiro watched the rise and fall of her breasts beneath the thin fabric of her top, captivated by the hypnotizing movement. Yuki became acutely aware of Hiro's prolonged gaze and felt flustered. Embarrassed, he shifted uneasily in his seat, fidgeting with his bento box contents. Glancing up once again, Hiro caught sight of Yuki's crimson cheeks and quickly redirected his attention elsewhere. Realizing he had been caught, Hiro feigned ignorance, pretending not to know why Momoko appeared flustered. Instead, he turned the topic to school matters, discussing an upcoming examination and offering advice to her in preparation. The change in subject helped alleviate some of Yuki's initial discomfort. He found himself enjoying Hiro's company as they discussed various topics, including their mutual interests in video games and literature.

The bell signaling the end of lunch break soon sounded, prompting the duo to gather their belongings. As they left the tranquil setting of the cherry tree-lined courtyard, a soft spring breeze caressed their faces, carrying with it a scent reminiscent of fresh beginnings.

"Don't forget we have swimming practice," Hiro reminded Momoko. "We need to get changed first." Nodding silently, Yuki began making his way toward the locker room. Adjusting his skirt carefully, he took slow measured steps, avoiding any unnecessary movements which might draw unwanted attention. Upon reaching the women's locker room, Yuki slipped quietly inside, trying to appear inconspicuous. Peering over his shoulder, Hiro noted the direction in which Momoko disappeared. As he entered the adjacent men's locker room, he couldn't help but glance longingly at the closed doors leading to the woman's dressing area.

Within the confines of the locker room, Yuki found himself surrounded by an array of energetic and focused individuals as he entered the space. Girls diligently preparing themselves for the upcoming practice session. Amidst the fervent chatter and unbridled giggles that filled the room, Yuki found himself standing alone, watching the others girls with a mixture of curiosity and confusion, normally it would be like a dream come true but he didn't feel any sexual desire towards these girls. Confused about these changes, Yuki retreated to a nearby bench, attempting to wrap his head around his sudden lack of interest in what previously held great appeal. Why didn't I find any of this appealing anymore? Yuki thought anxiously. Has my perception somehow altered due to my transformation into Momoko? Yuki questioned internally.

Suddenly, a girl came closer, addressing him directly. "Is everything okay, Momoko? You should start getting ready too." suggested the concerned girl.

Looking in her direction, he recognize Rika, one of the game's secondary characters and one of Momoko's friends. She was already wear her swimsuit and ready to leave. Seeing the confused look on Momoko's face, Rika decided to approach her friend.

"Everything's fine, thank you," Yuki answered, struggling to suppress his rising panic. Trying to put on a brave front, he forced a smile onto his face, hoping that his expression wouldn't betray his inner turmoil. Unable to hide his concern entirely, Yuki struggled to maintain eye contact with Rika, instead choosing to avert his gaze towards the floor. Swallowing hard, he mustered a weak response, saying, "Ah, yes... Just feeling a bit off today, perhaps." The lie did little to quell Rika's suspicion. Although she knew something wasn't quite right with Momoko, she respected her privacy enough not to press further. "Well, don't push yourself then, alright?" Rika finally offered kindly, giving Momoko a reassuring pat on the shoulder before departing.

Once Rika had gone, Yuki slowly start undressing, removing his school uniform piece by piece. First, he removed his blazer, followed by his button-up shirt. The air surrounding him was cooler than expected, causing goosebumps to surface across his skin. Shivering slightly, Yuki pulled off his skirt, exposing his legs clad in white and green stripped underwear. Exhaling audibly, he proceeded to remove his bra, leaving only his panties remaining. He then take off his undergarments, standing there in all his bare glory. Yuki felt embarrassment creeping up on him as he realized how vulnerable he was without any clothes on.

He then proceeded to don his school swimsuit, struggling with the task due to his ample chest size. "How does Momoko manage this ? isn't it her swimsuit ?" Yuki wondered to himself as he try to squeeze his breasts into the school-issued swimsuit. It fit snugly against his larger-than-average chest, causing him slight discomfort. adjusting the bottom part of the suit, Yuki tried to minimize the sensation of tightness around his groin. But no matter how much he tried, he could still feel the material rubbing against his sensitive areas.

As he emerged from the locker room, he saw Hiro waiting patiently for him. Smiling warmly, Hiro remarked "Hey Momoko! That swimsuit looks really nice on you!" Unconsciously, Yuki blushed, his gaze drifting downwards towards Hiro's own attire—a simple pair of blue swimming trunks. Surprised by his reaction, Yuki refocused his eyes back upon Hiro's face, finding him grinning playfully. "Thanks... uh..." he managed awkwardly, unable to think of anything else to say. Yuki suddenly noticed a growing bulge forming in Hiro's trunks, drawing his attention to it involuntarily. Flushing red with embarrassment, Yuki looked away quickly, clearing his throat nervously. Meanwhile, Hiro's bulging member seemed to grow even larger beneath his swim trunks, sending shivers of excitement down Yuki's spine. Intrigued yet hesitant, Yuki allowed his eyes to wander downwards again, unable to resist taking note of Hiro's physical attributes. With his heart racing, Yuki couldn't believe the intense urges beginning to well up within him. Feeling increasingly aroused by Hiro's burgeoning erection, Yuki made a conscious effort to contain his growing desire. However, the temptation proved too strong. Taking a cautious step forward, Yuki leaned in close to Hiro, "Let's get somewhere else", he murmured seductively, his voice a husky whisper.

Hiro nodded eagerly, grasping Yuki's hand and pulling him towards a secluded spot underneath a nearby maple tree. Its leaves rustled softly overhead, casting dancing patterns of sunlight amidst its branches. Once settled, Hiro released Yuki's hand, running his fingers along Momoko's collarbone until reaching the base of her neck. Drawing her closer, he tenderly kissed her earlobe. Yuki let out a soft moan, reveling in the gentle touch of Hiro's tongue teasing the shell of her ear. With each passing moment, their passion intensified. Unable to control himself any longer, Hiro reached for the hem of Momoko's swimsuit, sliding his hands up her thighs. The sensation sent shockwaves throughout Yuki's body, triggering a surge of anticipation deep within his core. Moans escaped Momoko's lips as Hiro cupped her firm ass, squeezing them gently. Her breath grew ragged as his finger traced circles just below her swimsuit's waistband, tantalizingly brushing against her exposed flesh.

Unperturbed by the sudden eroticism, Hiro continued his exploration, trailing his thumb along the top edge of Momoko's swimsuit, stopping just below her navel.

As he moved higher, his index finger teased the underside of her breast, delving dangerously close to her aching nipple. Closing his eyes, Yuki savored the exquisite sensation building within him. Hiro's hands expertly navigated the contours of Momoko's body, evoking euphoric responses that were beyond Yuki's wildest imagination. His fingertips grazed ever so lightly over the damp fabric covering her most intimate places, igniting newfound desires in Yuki. With each movement, his touch elicited moans and gasps of pleasure from Momoko. As if entranced, neither of them could deny the magnetic pull guiding their bodies together. Yuki could hear the rapid beat of his own heart, echoing loudly in his ears as Hiro's fingers glided along the length of Momoko's swimsuit, gradually moving lower towards her mound. Yuki felt a wave of heat rush through his entire body, his cheeks flaming hot as he imagined what lay ahead. Hiro's fingers deftly dipped beneath the thin barrier of Momoko's swimsuit, caressing her wet folds teasingly. A shiver ran down

Yuki's spine as he watched Hiro's hand continue its journey, skillfully spreading her open. Desperate to reach the source of such intensity, Hiro began to explore deeper, probing ever closer to her center. Each subtle nudge brought forth another moan of delight from Momoko's lips.

Yuki's body trembled with excitement as Hiro slipped two fingers deep inside her folds, stroking and circling her entrance, teasing her opening. Momoko's breath became shallow and irregular. Watching closely, Hiro carefully inserted a third finger alongside the first two, stretching her wider apart. This action caused waves of ecstatic agony to coursed through Momoko's frame, causing her to bite her lip, the pain transforming rapidly into raw desire.

Feeling overcome by his own lustful hunger, Hiro positioned himself behind Momoko, aligning his erect manhood with her dripping entrance. Gripping her hips firmly, he pressed his tip against her moist entrance, eliciting a sharp cry of anticipation from Momoko.

With every slow thrust, Hiro plunged deeper into Momoko's wet depths, allowing her body to adapt to his invasion. Their rhythm soon found its natural pace, each powerful stroke driving both partners toward the summit of pleasure. As they rocked back and forth, Yuki held Momoko steady, his arms wrapped securely around her waist. Every thrust drove him deeper, bringing them both nearer to satisfaction. Momoko's cries of joy grew louder, filling the air around them with the heady scent of sexual arousal. The tempo increased, propelling them towards their shared peak. Each motion brought the couple closer to culminating the fierce passion they'd built together. Hiro could sense the impending release gathering strength within Momoko, mirrored by his own mounting fervor. With a final thrust, he poured everything into one last powerful surge. Momoko's eyes rolled back in ecstasy, her mouth falling open in silent awe as the climax consumed her. Her insides contracted violently around Hiro's penetrating tool, milking him dry with every contraction. Overwhelmed by the sheer force of Momoko's orgasm, Hiro lost himself in her embrace, joining her in the abyss of ecstasy.

The aftershocks of their union left both of them quivering and spent, nestling comfortably in each other's arms. As they caught their breath, Momoko rested her head lovingly upon Hiro's shoulder while he stroked her hair affectionately. They stayed like that for several minutes, enjoying the quietude that surrounded them.

As Yuki's emotion gradually began to settle,he feel an overwhelming sense of unease. He could feel something distinctly off about himself; the boundary separating him from Momoko had become blurred. His thoughts were no longer purely his own, and he couldn't shake the sensation that he was losing control over his mind.

Panicked, Yuki struggled to break free from Hiro', only succeeding when He shifted slightly, releasing him from the protective embrace of his arms. Stumbling to his feet, Yuki hastily arrange his swimsuit before hurriedly turning away from the bewildered look in Hiro's eyes.

"Momoko," Hiro called hesitantly, but Yuki did not stop walking. There was a mixture of confusion and longing in his expression.

As Yuki walked back to the changing rooms, he couldn't help but wonder why he hadn't been able to stop things from happening the way they did. His body felt heavy and unwieldy, as though he wasn't entirely in control anymore. The thought terrified him – what if this loss of control extended to all aspects of his life? What would happen then? These questions whirled around in his head, leaving him feeling disoriented and anxious.

Back at the changing rooms, Yuki stripped off his swimsuit and showered quickly, hoping to rid himself of some of these disturbing thoughts. After dressing once more, he stood there alone, contemplating the events that transpired earlier. It appeared he didn't have much choice in how things unfolded today. But still, there was a nagging feeling of uncertainty lingering in his gut - a fear that perhaps fate had already chosen his path without giving him any room to deviate. And now, he was powerless to change the direction of this destiny.

As he considered these possibilities, he heard footsteps approaching. Turning, Yuki noticed Rika heading straight towards him.

"What's wrong, Momoko?" she asked, taking notice of his troubled expression.

Rika knew full well that Momoko often hid her true feelings from others, but even for her, today seemed different. She approached him with concern evident in her gaze. "Is something bothering you, Momoko?" she repeated, seeking confirmation.

Taking a deep breath, Yuki forced a small smile onto his face. "Just thinking too much," he replied lightly, attempting to deflect attention from his internal turmoil. 'Everything's fine.' However, Rika saw right through his façade. "It's alright, Momoko. I can tell something's going on. We're friends, remember?" Reaching out, she placed a consoling hand on his arm.

"You know you can always talk to me, right?" Rika said warmly, offering support. Though Momoko appreciated her understanding nature, he feared confiding in her might bring complications. After all, who could possibly understand what he experienced? Even discussing the matter with someone else might raise doubts about his sanity. No, it was better not to share these concerns. Yuki decided to put on a brave front despite his anxiety. Smiling faintly, he answered, "No worries, Rika. Just some stuff on my mind." Relieved, Rika let go of her initial worry. However, she still looked concerned. "Don't keep everything bottled up, okay? Remember, we're here for each other." Rika reminded softly, placing a gentle hand on his shoulder. Her gesture provided a measure of comfort.

"Anyway, I should probably return to the pool, I'll tell the teacher you were feeling under the weather," offered Rika kindly. "Before I forgot, Hiro asked if you could meet him on the roof after class, what should I tell him ?"Rika inquires calmly.

"Oh yes! Sure, just tell him I will be there." replies Yuki, trying hard to regain composure amidst his chaotic thoughts.

"Okay, I'll pass the message along. Take care, Momoko!" Rika says, showing genuine concern.

"Thanks, Rika. You too!" Yuki responds absentmindedly, stepping out of the locker room and disappearing into the hallways. Meanwhile, Rika watches Yuki leave, wondering whether there truly was anything troubling him.

Yuki wondered where he could find solitude to sort through his thoughts. Seeking refuge from his growing anxieties, he made his way outside and sat underneath a tree by the edge of the campus grounds. Gazing absently at the sky above, he tried to ignore the strange stirring within him.

CHANGING FEELINGS

Under the cool shade of a cherry blossom tree, Yuki brooded deeply. The sun cast a warm glow across the vast expanse of the school's beautiful garden. Unable to dispel the thoughts invading his consciousness, he leaned back against the trunk of the tree, letting its rough surface press into his skin, drawing his focus momentarily away from his inner torment. Yuki sighed heavily, closing his eyes briefly as he sought respite from the burden bearing down on him. In that moment, the rustling leaves overhead whispered soothing promises of serenity. Closing his eyes, Yuki allowed his racing thoughts to slow down, focusing instead on the calming sounds surrounding him. For once, he hoped the peace he sought wouldn't prove fleeting.

The sound of footsteps breaking the silence nearby snapped him back to reality. Opening his eyes, Yuki saw a tall boy standing beside him, glancing curiously at the solitary figure beneath the cherry blossom tree. Recognizing him as Taro, one of the male characters in the game and a friend of Hiro, had a reputation among students for being kind-hearted, gentle, and supportive toward those who crossed paths with him during their journey. With his expressive green eyes and tousled dark hair, many girls found themselves attracted to his charismatic demeanor. Yuki mustered a weak smile, offering a brief greeting. "Hi..." he uttered tentatively, struggling to compose himself as he watched Taro take a seat beside him. Taro returned the favor, smiling sympathetically. "It seems like you've got quite a bit on your mind, Momoko." Taro observed perceptively. Yuki nodded sheepishly, averting his gaze from Taro's intense scrutiny. Taro reached out, placing a reassuring hand on Yuki's shoulder. The sudden touch sent a wave of panic coursing through Yuki's veins.

Before he could process his alarm, Taro spoke softly, assuaging his unease. "Relax, Momoko. Sometimes our minds wander far beyond the boundaries of our own selves."

Intrigued, Yuki turned his gaze back towards Taro, questioningly awaiting further explanation.

Intrigued, Yuki admitted, "To be honest, lately, it feels like I am living two lives simultaneously ... One in which I feel completely detached from myself, lost, confused."

Taro listened intently, understanding only too well the confusion that comes with dual existences. He empathized with Yuki's struggle, knowing that navigating two worlds – one tangible and familiar, the other ethereal yet bewildering – required immense mental fortitude.

Staring at the verdant landscape stretched before them, Taro continued his counsel, saying earnestly, "Remember, Momoko, whatever happens in either existence doesn't define who you are. They coexist side by side, enriching rather than diminishing each other." He added solemnly. "But no matter how confusing things get, always remember - nothing changes who you really are at heart." Taro consoled gently.

Yuki felt somewhat relieved listening to Taro, but couldn't shake off the lingering fear. It seemed impossible not to succumb to his newfound desires; the constant whispers of forbidden temptations echoed deep within his soul. And yet, Yuki knew he must resist these urges; if he didn't, it would threaten his fragile hold on sanity. But despite his best efforts, images of Hiro and their encounters flashed through his mind. It was becoming increasingly difficult to deny what his body craved. Despite every attempt to push them aside, the memories of Hiro surfaced time and again. These thoughts were not merely sexual fantasies; they were intertwined with feelings of affection, trust, and longing. It wasn't just about satisfying base desires but something deeper, more profound. Yuki couldn't ignore the way his heart raced whenever he thought of Hiro, even though he tried. Feeling overwhelmed by conflicting emotions, Yuki let out a heavy sigh and leaned back against the tree once more.

Taro sensed the turmoil within Yuki, and decided to change the subject.Shifting closer to him under the canopy of the cherry blossoms, he asked, "So, did you know there's someone else here in the school?" Yuki raised an eyebrow quizzically. "What do you mean? There must be lots of people around," he replied cautiously. Taro smiled broadly, a hint of mischief sparkling in his eyes. "Not exactly..."

Without warning, Taro moved closer to Yuki, who instinctively stiffened in response. As they stood there together under the shelter of the cherry blossom tree, the scent of the flowers drifted past.

"But I said to much!" Taro joked nervously, breaking the heavy atmosphere as he realized he might have shared more information than planned. Noticing Yuki's growing inquiries, he offered up a playful grin. "Don't worry about it, Momoko! Anyway, I have to go now." Said Taro, as he stood up, turning to leave.

The colorful petals fell gracefully from above, casting a delicate pattern onto the ground below. Unwilling to lose sight of Taro's presence, Yuki hesitated, looking up at him uncertainly. Their conversation had been filled with intrigue, leaving Yuki wondering whether he should pursue the topic further. In the briefest moment, as Yuki closed his eyes for an instant, he found that Taro had vanished into thin air. Yuki rose swiftly to his feet, searching frantically amidst the sea of cherry blossoms. Yet despite all his efforts, Taro remained hidden. The wind rustled through the trees, carrying faint traces of sweet perfume borne upon the tender breeze. The setting sun painted the sky hues of orange and crimson, casting a golden light on the remaining blooming petals scattered across the school grounds.Yuki walked slowly, taking in the tranquility of his surroundings. This environment served as a stark contrast to the chaotic whirlwind swirling within his mind. He contemplated Taro's departure, feeling slightly disoriented without any answers.

Turning to walk towards the path leading to the building, he noticed movement from the corner of his eye. To his surprise, a petite girl with raven black hair emerged from behind a cluster of cherry blossom trees. She carried herself with an undeniable sense of confidence and poise, her piercing emerald eyes meeting his directly. Yuki recognized her instantly—it was Yumi, one of the love interests in the game Waku Waku Romance. Standing tall and proud before him, she exuded an unmistakable charm and confidence. The girl approached him calmly, her elegant movements seemingly effortless.

"Hello, Momoko," she addressed with a soft voice. Caught off guard, Yuki managed a feeble reply, "Ah, hi..."

"Hello, Momoko," she repeated, extending her slender fingers to brush her fingertips against his cheek, eliciting a shiver from Yuki involuntarily. Yumi then pulled back, maintaining a respectful distance between them.

"Is everything alright, Momoko?" She queried, concern etched plainly across her features.

Embarrassed by his wandering thoughts, Yuki cleared his throat awkwardly. "Yes, um... Everything's fine." He lied hastily, averting his eyes. "Thank you for asking, but yes, everything is alright," he stammered, struggling to regain composure. His heart still thumped wildly against his ribcage while sweat trickled down his brow. Yumi looked at him quizzically, observing his agitation with a keen curiosity. Something told her that something significant happened earlier, but Momoko remained tightlipped, unwilling to divulge anything regarding his internal struggles. Still, she found solace in the fact that Momoko appeared relatively normal, if not slightly distracted. Regardless, Yumi couldn't dismiss the odd mannerisms of Momoko, particularly due to the unusual encounter with Taro moments ago. Whatever transpired had left a noticeable impact on her.

After a few seconds of silence, Yuki took advantage of the opportunity to ask about Taro. "By the way, Yumi," began Yuki carefully,

"Do you happen to know where Taro went?" Yumi hesitated briefly, choosing her words deliberately. "I don't think anyone knows exactly where he goes." Yumi answered nonchalantly. "He tends to disappear sometimes." Replied Yumi, giving a slight shrug of her shoulders. Then, as if suddenly recalling some detail, she paused for a second, a curious glint in her eye. Turning toward the nearby school buildings, she murmured, "There's someone you need to speak with, isn't there?" Momoko nodded silently, acknowledging her intuition. "Yes, Hiro is waiting for me on the roof right now," he uttered, his tone indicating mixed emotions. With apprehension and excitement simmering beneath the surface, Yuki steeled himself, preparing to confront the complexities of his feelings for Hiro head-on.

As Yuki departed, Yumi watched him thoughtfully. Something about the exchange with Taro troubled her deeply.

Yuki could hardly contain his emotional stat as he made his way to meet Hiro. Caught up in the whirlwind of conflicting emotions that stemmed from his duality, Momoko found herself irresistibly attracted to Hiro, who had become both a close confidant and a possible romantic interest. As Yuki, however, he struggled with the uncertainty surrounding his own identity, fearing that if he allowed himself to fully embrace these feelings, he might lose sight of who he truly was. This internal conflict weighed heavily on him, leaving him grappling for answers amidst the turmoil within. He longed for clarity, desperately seeking a way to reconcile his two distinct personas into one cohesive whole.

Gathering his courage, he ascended the steps to the rooftop, his determination to confront Hiro apparent in his resolute strides. Upon reaching the top floor, he take a deep breath and open the door.

CONFESSION

When Yuki arrived at the rooftop, he couldn't help but feel awestruck by the magnificence of the panoramic view that stretched out before him. The city lights twinkled like stars dotting the horizon, punctuating the nighttime sky. Gazing upon this celestial canvas, Yuki felt a sense of serenity envelop him. Gingerly stepping forward, he crossed the threshold into the illuminated space.

As his gaze fixed upon Hiro, standing motionlessly against the moonlit skyline, his heart quickened its pace. Hiro greeted Yuki warmly, offering him a smile radiating confidence and comfort. Even though Yuki felt overwhelmed by his burgeoning feelings, he couldn't help but return the gesture, finding reassurance in Hiro's friendly demeanour. Drawing nearer, Yuki felt a wave of heat rising within him, causing his face to flush. He clutched the hem of his skirt, attempting to steady his nerves. Breathing deeply, Yuki reminded himself that facing his feelings was necessary - especially considering how complicated things were becoming.

Hiro stepped forward, closing the gap between them."You look beautiful tonight, Momoko." He whispered intimately, reaching for her hand with tenderness, only to have her pull away timidly. Feeling embarrassed yet drawn to Hiro's affection, Yuki tried hard to remain composed. "Tha.. Thank you, Hiro," he responded sheepishly, managing a weak smile as he attempted to diffuse the situation. His pulse raced furiously, betraying his inner turmoil. Emotions tangled within him, tearing him apart as reality began to set in.

It became increasingly clear to Yuki that his struggle would ultimately determine which version of himself dominated – the introverted loner in the virtual world or the lovestruck girl in this newfound reality. It was a crossroads he never imagined traversing. However, as his hands reached instinctively for Hiro's, the decision seemed to make itself. The weight of his confusion eased somewhat, as he realized he didn't want to deny the attraction he felt. Letting go of any reservations, Yuki leaned closer to Hiro, wrapping his arms around him gently.

"Momoko..." Hiro started, speaking tenderly with sincerity. "I want to tell you something important. I'm in love whith you," Hiro said earnestly, gazing deeply into her eyes. Yuki's heart skipped a beat, warmed by the genuine sentiment expressed in those simple words.

Unable to suppress his desire any longer, he moved forward, pressing his lips firmly against Hiro's.

"Whenever we're together like this," Yuki began, softly caressing Hiro's cheek, "I feel so different than my usual self. It's almost as if I've finally found what I've been searching for all along." Yuki admitted, his voice trembling slightly, a faint blush appearing on his cheeks. "To be honest, I've never experienced anything quite like this before... And it scares me just a little bit," he added, his eyes searching Hiro's gaze for understanding. Hiro gave him a gentle squeeze, reassuring him with a tender kiss. "Don't worry, Momoko. Whatever happens, you'll always be yourself. We can explore our relationship without compromising your true identity." Hiro assured Yuki confidently, stroking his back gently. "And even if things get difficult sometimes, remember that you aren't alone. I will always be here for you." Yuki took solace in Hiro's assurances, allowing some of the anxiety to dissipate from his chest. Nodding gratefully, he embraced Hiro once more, grateful for the support. Their hearts synchronized, beating rhythmically as their bodies melted into each other.

Yuki let go of any lingering doubts, succumbing to the magnetic force pulling them together. Their lips met again, tongues dancing eagerly across one another's mouths. Intense sensations coursed through every fiber of their being, consuming them entirely. The cool evening breeze brushed against their flushed skin, sending shivers down their spines. Yuki closed his eyes, surrendering completely to the erotic thrill coursing through his veins. With every passing moment, his fear of losing control faded further behind, replaced instead by an insatiable craving for closeness. He had fallen hopelessly in love with Hiro, body and soul, consumed by a burning desire for physical connection. Hiro's touch ignited sparks within him, setting off waves of euphoria throughout his entire frame. Each brush of Hiro's fingers sent ripples of pleasure coursing through Yuki's core, intensifying the throbbing ache beneath his clothes. Unable to resist the urge, Yuki guided Hiro's hand towards his crotch, eliciting a smoldering groan from the depths of his lustful heart.

Hiro palpably swelled underneath his pants, creating a delicious friction as their hips ground against each other. Tenderly, Yuki slipped his tongue between Hiro's lips, probing gently until their tongues entwined effortlessly. Each wet lap made their desires escalate. With a fierce determination born from his yearning, Yuki grasped onto Hiro's shoulders tightly, drawing him even closer. As their bodies pressed together, his breathing grew labored in anticipation. Every point of contact brought forth an unparalleled level of stimulation. Yuki moaned softly as Hiro explored every curve of his body, tracing patterns along his back, up and down his thighs, lingering near his entrance. Both of them grew increasingly aroused, struggling to maintain composure amidst their mounting excitement. The air thickened with raw desire, amplified by the heady mixture of sweat and pheromones filling the atmosphere. Neither Yuki nor Hiro could contain themselves any longer. With nimble fingers, Yuki undid the buttons on Hiro's pants, lowering them slowly to expose his throbbing erection. As it sprang free, Yuki wrapped his slim fingers around Hiro's shaft, marveling at the velvety smoothness of his flesh. He stroked the length carefully, reveling in the sensual act, glancing up to meet Hiro's deepening gaze. Hiro returned the favor, fondling Momoko's breast softly, gently pinching her nipple.

Her breath caught, a small cry escaping her lips involuntarily. As their movements quickened, she felt Hiro reach under her skirt, parting her folds, probing deeper into her drenched core. Moans escaped her lips as she pushed herself harder against him, taking in every stroke of his expert fingerwork. Unbridled pleasure shot through her system, leaving her weak and pleasantly disoriented. Yuki felt helpless against the force of his desire. As his body trembled in response to the intensity of their encounter, he pulled Hiro close, sharing an achingly intimate embrace. Yuki savored the taste of Hiro's lips as their tongues entwined, the pressure building steadily within him. Desire blazed within his loins, prompting him to shift position, He turn around and bent over slowly, allowing his arms to rest gently against the cool surface of the nearby wall. Embracing his new role fully, Yuki arched his back, thrusting his hips suggestively as he allowed his skirt to slide ever higher up his legs. Exposed and vulnerable, his skin quivered with nervous anticipation, heightening the overall effect of his sensuous display. The musky fragrance of sexual desire filled the air.

Grasping Yuki's hips tightly, Hiro drove his cock into Momoko's awaiting folds, impaling her slowly but surely. Momoko gasped audibly, a mix of pain and ecstatic release flashing across her features. As he continued his descent, Hiro paused briefly, letting Momoko adjust to the fullness before plunging deeper still. The intensity of his penetration caused Momoko to bite her lip, trying to subdue the agonizing sweetness of submission. Hiro matched her pace, surging in and out of her, the motion deliberately slow. His relentless rhythm kept Momoko teetering on the edge of satisfaction, tantalizing her senses mercilessly. Gradually, his pace increased, driving her toward a peak that threatened to consume her entirely. Her breath came in ragged gasps, each contraction bringing her ever closer to complete oblivion. With every push of Hiro's pelvis, Momoko felt her walls flex, preparing to accept him fully.

The intense friction created a spiraling vortex of pleasure within her core, threatening to pull her consciousness away. She clenched her teeth in resistance against the building wave of ecstasy. Her labia welcomed him warmly, milking his cock greedily with each invading thrust. Hiro seized upon this opportunity, accelerating his pace, pounding into her, faster, harder, pushing her limits to the absolute breaking point. Momoko's breaths turned shallow and erratic, her entire focus now concentrated solely on the exquisite torture of Hiro's persistent advance. Momoko's body shook violently as a powerful orgasm ripped through her. Crying out loudly, she convulsed wildly, bucking hard against Hiro's own furious pace. Clutching her tightly, he rode her relentlessly, his cock hitting her pleasure button perfectly. Each time, she would call out his name, either in encouragement or utter joy. Her cries were music to his ears, a testament to how much she enjoyed what was happening. He held himself high enough to ensure that every stroke hit that magical spot deep inside her. His thrusts were steady and purposeful, moving her in ways no one else ever had before.

Their bodies writhed against each other, the sounds of their moans echoing through the night sky. Hiro's hands roamed possessively over Momoko's curves, as his thumb circled her clit, causing her to gasp and squirm in delight. As Hiro continued his relentless assault on Momoko's innocence, the lines between reality and fantasy - between Yuki and Momoko became irrevocably blurred, merging together in perfect harmony. As each thrust brought her closer to climax, Momoko felt a sharp twinge in her perineum. Hiro reached down to caress it tenderly, adding another layer of sensation that left her unable to think straight. She threw her head back, abandoning all pretense of modesty, giving way to primal instincts. Her hips bucked wildly, meeting his thrusts in perfect sync. Each movement sent waves of pure delight crashing through her. The tenderness with which Hiro touched her, coupled with the ferocity of his assault, was unlike anything she'd ever experienced before. It was almost as though his hands knew exactly where to press, sending shockwaves of pleasure coursing through her. As Momoko neared the precipice yet again, Hiro began to pick up speed, his thrusts becoming more forceful, driving her deeper into the abyss of ecstasy. As Hiro reached his peak, the intensity of the ecstasy he bestowed upon her became all-consuming, much like an unstoppable tsunami of euphoria. The sensation coursed through every fiber of her body, leaving her dazed and utterly overwhelmed by the sheer magnitude of the experience. Momoko couldn't help but scream Hiro's name once more, as her body tightened, pulsing with an electric charge.

Momoko fell limply onto the wall, breathless and dazed. Her cheeks flushed red as she struggled to regain her bearings. Emotionally spent, physically exhausted, and mentally reeling from the sheer intensity of their encounter, Momoko leaned heavily against the cool stone wall, her heart racing incessantly. Staring out into the night sky, a million stars gleaming faintly above, she tried to catch her breath. Still flush with excitement, adrenaline pumping through her veins, she wondered if she should say something, break the silence. But nothing seemed appropriate after such an earthshaking encounter. Instead, they simply stood there, lost in thought, tangible evidence of their passion lying crumbled on the floor. Finally, she mustered the courage to speak, her voice wavering slightly. "That...was incredible." He nodded in agreement, mirroring her sentiment. "Yes, indeed," he murmured, brushing his hand lightly in her pink hair. In a momentary lapse of self-consciousness, Momoko let go of any pretenses, allowing herself to feel truly vulnerable in front of Hiro. "Thank you..." she whispered hesitantly, searching for words to express just how deeply he affected her. He smiled softly, capturing her face gently in his palms, guiding her towards him. "It's my pleasure." Their faces inches apart, they locked eyes for several moments, each seemingly willing the other to make the first move. Yet neither could quite bring themselves to do so. His touch sent a wave of affection rippling through her, intensifying her connection with him. Gingerly reaching for his hand, she intertwined their fingers, feeling strangely comforted by the simple gesture.

The moonlight cast an ethereal glow over them, bathing them both in a warm luminescence. Silence hung heavy in the air, punctuated only by the occasional rustle of leaves.

As minutes passed without further discussion, Momoko found herself gradually relaxing beneath the weight of Hiro's protective arm, nestled snugly against his side.

A sense of peace and tranquility settled over her, as if the storm of passion subsided, replaced instead by serene calm. Even as the warmth of Hiro's embrace enveloped her, a sudden shiver ran down her spine, stirring memories long buried within the depths of her soul.

"Are you cold?" Hiro asked concernedly, noticing her slight tremble.

She nodded, her breath forming tiny clouds in the chilly night air. "Just a little bit," she admitted sheepishly.

"We should probably make our way home soon. It's getting late," said Hiro, glancing down at his watch. Though part of him wanted to stay wrapped up in her warm embrace forever, the practicality of reality demanded action. Together, they started walking back towards their homes.

As the wind swept past, blowing wisps of her hair gently around her face, Momoko couldn't help but smile contentedly. There was something undeniably comforting about having someone beside her who understood and accepted her for who she really was – imperfections and all. For once, she didn't feel compelled to hide behind her usual facade, nor did she fear judgement from those around her. For some reason, Hiro made her feel comfortable in her skin. Walking along the quiet streets under the starry night sky, she noticed how vivid everything appeared—the contrast of colors stood out even more than usual, creating a dreamlike atmosphere. This newfound closeness with Hiro gave her a profound appreciation for the small things in life, a subtle shift in perspective that opened doors previously hidden to her.

As they strolled leisurely along, the sound of their footsteps synchronized in a gentle rhythm, matching the cadence of their heartbeats. Hiro slid his arms around Momoko's waist, pulling her close. Nestled securely in his embrace, Momoko felt safe, protected. The warmth of his body radiated throughout hers, easing her lingering discomfort. Lost in the magic of the nighttime stroll, they navigated the dimly lit street, occasionally passing underneath lampposts whose flickering lights danced across their faces. Despite their height difference, Momoko somehow managed to fit comfortably into Hiro's embrace, her delicate frame curled against his solid form. With each step forward, she grew increasingly aware of the steady beat of his heart thudding steadfastly against her ear.

After a few minutes of walking together, they eventually arrived at the gate leading to Momoko's house. Turning to face him, she took his hands in hers, smiling shyly. Unable to resist, Hiro pulled her closer, pressing his lips against hers. Momoko closed her eyes, allowing herself to fully surrender to the moment.

As their lips parted, Hiro spoke softly, brushing away a loose strand of hair from her face. "Goodnight, Momoko." The word rolled off his tongue like velvet, sending shivers down her spine. She responded with a similar sweetness, wrapping her arms around his neck and nuzzling into his shoulder. "Goodnight, Hiro," she replied dreamily, her voice low and seductive.

He watched her walk toward her door, her hips swaying hypnotically with each step. He could see her reflection in the window, her silhouette casting a stark contrast against the darkness outside. Hiro remained rooted to the spot, mesmerized by the sight of her retreating figure.

Upon reaching the door, Momoko paused briefly to look back over her shoulder, catching Hiro's gaze. She gently opened the door, taking one last lingering glance at the moonlit sky, before stepping indoors.

Once safely ensconced within the walls of her house, Momoko kicked off her shoes, letting them fall haphazardly to the ground.

Closing the door quietly behind her, she tiptoed across the wooden flooring. Unbidden, her feet led her directly to her bedroom, where she promptly shed her clothes. Standing naked before her full-length mirror, she examined her reflection critically, admiring the curves and contours of her newly acquired womanhood. She traced the outline of her pert breasts with her fingertips, marveling at the change they had wrought upon her. Closing her eyes, she remembered Hiro's hungry gaze during their passionate tryst earlier tonight, the way his hands roamed eagerly over her body, possessively claiming it as his own. The memory brought forth a blush to her cheeks, which she quickly suppressed.

After completing her tasks around the house, she felt weary yet satisfied with what she had accomplished throughout the day. It was now time to relax and unwind in the bath, relishing the warmth of the water and the luxurious foams caressing her skin. Carefully positioning herself in the tub, she eased her aching muscles, indulging in the pampering bubbles. The sensation of the suds lazily drizzling down her body filled her with a pervasive sense of well-being. As the heat rose and dissipated, she observed her pale complexion transform into a rosy glow.

Feeling invigorated yet tender, she climbed out of the tub, slowly drying herself with the plush, white towel.

Stepping into her room, she donned a pair of satiny white panties, slipping effortlessly onto her smooth, silky skin. Next came a pink chemise that

accentuated her ample bosom, followed by a pair of fluffy, cloud-soft pajama bottoms.

Slumping down onto her bed, she propped

her pillow against the headboard, resting her weary head upon it.

Thoughts of Hiro filled her mind, his image superimposed upon her

mental landscape. Her heart raced at the mere idea of seeing him again tomorrow, a fluttery anticipation rising within her chest.

Sleep proved elusive, though, as she lay awake tossing and turning beneath the sheets. Her body still buzzed with energy, her blood thrummed with excitement, coursing hotly through her veins. All too conscious of her arousal, she shifted restlessly, trying to seek relief from the persistent throbbing deep within her core. Eventually, exhaustion overtook her, dragging her into the dark abyss of sleep.

YUKI AND MOMOKO

In her subconscious state, dreams began to take shape - dreams of her old life as Yuki, juxtaposed against her new existence as Momoko. The two personas merged seamlessly, their individual qualities merging harmoniously together. The two sides of her nature coexisted within the same physical vessel, complementing rather than conflicting with one another.Still dreaming, she found herself gazing into a mirror, expecting to see her own reflection staring back at her. But much to her surprise, what greeted her eyes wasn't her own image; rather, it was that of Yuki.His face looked eerily familiar, etched with an expression of vulnerability and confusion.

"What..." she muttered groggily. She then reached tentatively towards her reflection, as if half convinced it might disappear were she to touch it.

As her fingers met Yuki's familiar face, a strange feeling swelled within her chest, causing goosebumps to break out across her skin. A wave of sadness crashed over her, coupled with guilt for leaving him stuck in such a situation. His eyes seemed pleading, imploring her to understand his predicament.

"Why?" he whispered hoarsely, his brow furrowed in bewilderment.

Momoko hesitated, unsure of how to approach this seemingly impossible conundrum. Finally, she summoned the courage to speak, her voice quivering slightly. "It isn't my fault," she said, hoping that her resolve would reach him even amidst his foggy disorientation. "This is no ordinary wish granted. My very essence was transformed."

"Then tell me, how do I return to normalcy? How can I get back home?" asked Yuki earnestly, clearly struggling to process the reality of his predicament.

Momoko paused, deeply troubled by the implications of her suggestion. Though sympathetic to his plight, there seemed little hope for salvaging his former identity – she was forever bound to these newfound limbs. "There may not be a solution." Her words echoed through the air, resonating heavily in both their hearts. "However, let us focus on enjoying our lives here." Momoko proposed cautiously, attempting to lighten the mood somewhat.

As she reached out her hand towards him, an unsteady expression crossed his face. He hesitated for a moment before finally mustering up the courage to accept her offer. His shaking fingers gently encircled her warm palm as he clasped onto it tightly. It took every ounce of determination within Momoko to pull him out of the mirror and onto the floor beside her. "Come, sit down," she instructed, gesturing towards the nearby bed. Upon sitting, he couldn't help but notice the delicious curve of her breast underneath the thin fabric of her top. His eyes involuntarily wandered lower, trailing along the gentle slope of her waist, eventually coming to rest on the soft rounded bulge of her thighs. Anxiety began to creep through him once more, causing his pulse to quicken and his breath to catch in his throat. Despite all odds stacked against him, he felt drawn irresistibly closer to her. This alien creature housing his soul fascinated him beyond measure—the curvatures of her form, the texture of her skin, the warmth emanating from her flesh, all held a mysterious appeal that captivated him completely.Even as his rationality tried desperately to regain control, he knew deep within himself that this foreign entity had taken root within his being, permanently altering who he was. There could be no escape, only adaptation, surrendering to this new existence. With a faint sigh, Yuki resigned himself to the present reality. Despite the inherent strangeness of this predicament, a part of him was grateful for the opportunity to experience life through Momoko's perspective, despite the difficulties posed by their dual existence. Even so, a nagging apprehension lingered somewhere within him — an anxiety regarding the future prospects of his true self. Would he ever reclaim ownership of his past life? Could they somehow manage to bridge the gap between their disparate existences, uniting them harmoniously? These questions loomed heavy in his mind, refusing to succumb to silence.

However, Momoko offered reassurance instead of answers, gently stroking his arm with her small hand. "Don't worry," she comforted. "In your new existence as Momoko, you will still maintain aspects of yourself. We simply need to adapt." Momoko spoke confidently, though her heart raced wildly beneath her ribcage. She longed to protect him, yet understood that they needed to explore this new reality together. "The first step is to acknowledge that we're now connected spiritually." Momoko explained, her hand reaching instinctively toward his shoulder.

Throughout this conversation, Yuki grew increasingly anxious about losing sight of his original identity, wondering whether he would ever truly feel whole again. However, Momoko tried her best to assuage his concerns, promising that they would figure things out together. Both were acutely aware of the significance of their intertwined fates, grasping at the tenuous threads that connected them spiritually. Their bond stretched far beyond the superficial, linking souls, minds, and bodies into a single coherent whole. Each sought validation and support in the other's presence, finding strength where once weakness prevailed. They embraced one another tenderly, accepting the unpredictable journey ahead.

Yuki felt an overwhelming sense of embarrassment as he found himself caught up in this intimate moment. His face turned a deep shade of red, reflecting his inner turmoil. The rapid beating of his heart betrayed his anxiety. Meanwhile, Momoko, sensing his discomfort, drew closer still, gently pressing her soft lips against the delicate skin of Yuki's cheek. Her tender gesture was meant to comfort him, yet it only served to heighten his unease.

He glanced nervously around, trying hard to ignore the sudden surge of arousal he felt whenever she came close. Embarrassed by his growing desire, he attempted to divert attention away from his erection, yet it stubbornly refused to diminish. Frustrated and confused, he struggled to reconcile his internal conflict. On one hand, he craved connection and understanding, whereas on the other, he feared succumbing entirely to this carnal attraction. Momoko noticed his discomfort, intuitively offering consolation through subtle gestures and kisses. Each embrace brought forth a mixture of passion and apprehension, further intensifying the erotic atmosphere surrounding them. Unable to resist the temptation any longer, Yuki reluctantly gave in to his urges, allowing himself to be engulfed by desire.

He leaned forward, brushing his lips softly against hers, slowly savoring the taste of her mouth. The blissful warmth enveloping him made it difficult to think rationally. Desire coursed through his veins like a fierce drug, propelling him blindly forward. His hands traced the contours of her body, exploring each tantalizing detail, reveling in the sensual pleasure of touch. The smell of her perfume intoxicated him further, dizzying his senses.

Momoko closed her eyes briefly, letting loose the suppressed moans which escaped her lips. In response, Yuki's hands roamed boldly, skimming over the supple curves of her hips and waist. He marveled at the smooth texture of her skin, unable to tear his eyes away from the undulating motion of her bosom. Her nipples stood firm, erect with

desire, drawing his touch almost instinctively. Intrigued by this discovery, he cupped her full mounds gently, eliciting an involuntary gasp from her lips. He moved his thumb over the rosy tip, teasing her sensitive nub. Surprised by his brazenness, Momoko squirmed slightly under his ministrations, eagerly encouraging him to continue. Her pupils dilated with excitement, reflecting the mounting intensity between them.

She leaned in, her tongue entwining with his own, inviting him deeper into their shared passion. His hands continued to explore her body, caressing her breasts, tracing the lines of her waist and sliding across her soft skin until he reached the edge of her clothes.

She looked upon him expectantly, her eyes filled with a mix of desire and curiosity.

Uncertainty flashed across Yuki's features - uncertainty coupled with burning passion. Yet something else too - confusion, fear. And guilt perhaps, buried deep below his conscious thought.

As if in response to the shift in atmosphere, Momoko reached out to stroke his chest affectionately, leaving goosebumps in her wake. Her soft touch incited a flood of feelings, igniting an intense yearning within him. She bent forward, grazing her lips gently against his neck, sending waves of electricity coursing through his entire frame.

Yuki trembled visibly, struggling to contain his rapidly escalating desire. Momoko wrapped her arms tightly around him, drawing him flush against her own lithe form. Her supple curves pressed snugly against his own, stirring a heady mix of anticipation and longing within him. He pulled her closer still, feeling her soft, silken hair cascade gently against his cheeks.

Their hearts beat synchronously, reflecting the rhythm of their fervent desires. As Yuki's hands explored the landscape of her curves, her soft gasps fueling his ardor, he discovered depths within himself previously unknown. He delved greedily into these newly-awakened passions, experiencing them not just with his body, but also with his mind and soul. Every sensation amplified his awareness of Momoko's very essence — the scent of her hair, the velvety texture of her skin, even the slight quiver of her voice when expressing her needs. It seemed as though every aspect of their encounter was imbued with meaning, as if their union transcended mere physical satisfaction, evolving into something profoundly spiritual.

Clothes flew off effortlessly, discarded carelessly in their haste to indulge in the most forbidden pleasures. Yuki ran his fingers down the length of Momoko's thigh, causing her breath to catch audibly. Gathering courage, he ventured lower, taking note of the way her muscles tensed lightly under his gentle touch. He circled the base of her navel, before moving lower again, his hands finally coming to rest on the swollen bud nestled between her legs.

Momoko bit her lip, her back arched slightly, her breath quickening. Her ample breasts bounced gently above him, held aloft by perky, rosebud nipples begging for his attention.

Despite the chaos reigning within his psyche, he couldn't help but observe the striking beauty of Momoko's body. Her perfectly sculpted, voluptuous breasts captivated him completely. With gentle movements, he stroked the soft flesh, admiring how her pale skin contrasted sharply with the dark pink of her nipples. Tenderly, he suckled on her right breast, circling the puckered tip with his tongue, eliciting a sultry groan from her throat.

Reciprocating, he allowed her to draw him into her soft embrace, massaging his cock gently with her hand. The slow, deliberate movement sent thrilling shockwaves through his core, causing his heartbeat to increase along with his desire.

His penis, now rock-hard, prodded insistently against her folds, demanding entrance. Despite his initial hesitation, Yuki followed suit, thrusting carefully into her wet, welcoming heat. Her hips bucked slightly, meeting his rhythmic strokes with perfect timing.

Her moans grew more intense, spiraling higher and higher, building into a crescendo of ecstasy. Her fingers curled into the sheets beneath them, digging furrows into the fabric. Momoko's body tensed and relaxed in a harmonious rhythm, mirroring Yuki's own movements.

Eager to prolong their shared experience, Yuki adjusted his position, wrapping his arms protectively around Momoko's smaller frame. The sensation of holding her so closely triggered unexpected emotional resonances within him, filling him with a newfound sense of tenderness. His eyes met hers, their gaze locking in mutual appreciation. This act of love became more than simply gratification; it transformed into an exchange of vulnerability, trust, and genuine connection.

With every undulation of their bodies, they surrendered themselves wholly to each other, merging their souls into a single, indivisible entity. Their hearts raced together, pounding with equal intensity, fueled by the power of their passion.The once separate entities merged seamlessly, losing all trace of individual boundaries. Their bodies, their minds, and their spirits became intertwined, creating a force far greater than either could have achieved alone. Each thrust drove them deeper into the vortex of unbridled lust, the two becoming indistinguishable from one another, their energy feeding off each other endlessly. They clung onto each other as the earth shattering climax approached, both knowing it would change their lives forever.

Their hearts raced faster, beating in tandem, the blood flowing hot through their veins. Time ceased to exist in this cocoon of intimacy. Lost in the haze of euphoria, swept up in the storm of passion, Yuki let go of everything except Momoko. As time slipped away, nothing mattered save for the sheer joy of being joined with her. As they moved towards climax, each thrust felt harder, more urgent than the last. Emotions surged forth in rapid succession, each wave crashing down on them without pause. Yuki cried out her name repeatedly, echoing her own growing exhortations, as if binding them irreversibly together. Her fingers dug deeply into his shoulders, her nails scratching him lightly, marking him indelibly as her own. They cried out loudly in sync, their orgasms crashing over them simultaneously, merging into one powerful wave of ultimate fulfillment.

In this moment, there were no longer barriers separating their selves; they had become inextricably linked, bound irrevocably together.Momoko, exhausted both physically and emotionally, collapsed into the mattress, alone.

REVELATIONS

Momoko stirred awake gradually, like an ocean wave gently lapping at the shore. Tears silently streamed down her cheeks, leaving wet trails on her pillowcase as she lay sprawled among rumpled sheets.

Her eyes, glazed over with sorrow, betrayed her emotional turmoil. Unable to hide her pain, she curled herself into a fetal position, attempting to comfort herself amidst the empty space left behind by Yuki.

Feeling utterly lost and abandoned, Momoko knew she needed solace. Reaching for her phone, she dialed a familiar number. "Hello?" came the faint voice from the other side. "Hi, it's me," she replied softly, trying to mask her distress. There was silence on the other end for a few moments, during which Momoko tried hard to compose herself. Finally, Hiro spoke, his voice full of concern. "What happened? Are you okay?"

Taking a deep breath, Momoko struggled to find words to describe what had taken place. "Nothing," she lied. "Just some bad dream." She said, fighting back tears threatening to spill over.

"It must have been quite a nightmare." Hiro responded sympathetically, hoping to ease Momoko's discomfort. "Do you want to talk about it?"

Momoko remained silent for several seconds, weighing whether to confide in him. "I don't know... maybe I should tell you..." she finally admitted tentatively. "But it wasn't just a dream..."

There was a brief silence on the line, as Hiro attempted to comprehend the gravity of the situation. Eventually, he spoke again, his tone concerned yet understanding. "Can you explain what happened?" asked Hiro quietly, fearful of pushing too quickly. Momoko took a deep breath before divulging her secret. "Okay," she whispered timidly, her brow creased with anxiety. It seemed impossible to discuss such a delicate subject over the phone, but Hiro understood her predicament. Nodding his head in acknowledgement, he continued to offer supportive reassurance. "Take your time. We can talk whenever you feel ready. "Momoko appreciated his nonjudgmental attitude, feeling grateful for having someone who truly cared for her well-being. "Thank you," she managed, stifling a sob, her voice breaking with suppressed emotion. "Can you come over here? Please?" She sniffled heavily after her request, waiting anxiously for a response. After a slight delay, Hiro confirmed, his voice gentle but resolute. "Of course, I'll be right over." Hiro assured Momoko warmly, already preparing himself mentally for whatever revelation awaited him upon arrival. Meanwhile, Momoko sat tensely on her bed, her mind swimming with memories of her life as Yuki. She remains motionless in this position for several minutes, her body language conveying an air of deep contemplation, before she start to get ready.

As she prepared herself for Hiro's impending visit, her mind raced with thoughts about what to wear, how to style her hair, even considering whether to paint her lips or not.

She took her time selecting an outfit, opting for something cute yet comfortable, reflecting her personality as Momoko. Her choice of attire consisted of a fluffy green mini skirt paired with a cropped white blouse featuring frilly sleeves. She styled her long locks neatly,

ensuring they framed her face gracefully. With each passing minute, her nervousness intensified, causing her hands to tremble slightly as she applied mascara and eyed shadow. All along, the image of Hiro's face loomed in her consciousness. As she finished applying lip gloss, stepping back to admire her reflection, she felt somewhat relieved.

A sudden, unexpected knock echoed through the house, causing her heart rate to skyrocket. Her palms grew clammy as adrenaline coursed through her veins. Taking deep breaths, she mustered all her strength and courage. Slowly, deliberately, she approached the door, grasping the handle firmly. Before opening it, she paused briefly to take a deep calming breath, steadying her nerves.

As the door began to open, she caught sight of the sun setting outside, casting a golden hue across the room. The rays illuminated Momoko's skin with a subtle warmth, highlighting her curves beneath her elegant ensemble. Her heart quickened involuntarily as she gazed at the man standing before her.

As the door fully opened, Hiro stood there, visibly shaken by the vulnerability she displayed. His eyes swept across her body appreciatively, taking note of her striking appearance, his heart racing in anticipation. Uncertainty hung heavy in the air as Momoko stepped aside, allowing Hiro entry into her home. He hesitantly followed suit, crossing the threshold into new territory – both physically and metaphorically.

Once inside, Momoko led them to her room, where the sunlight filtered in through the windows, painting the room with a soothing ambiance. Both awkwardly took seats opposite one another, unsure of how to proceed with their conversation.Silence settled thickly around them, filled only by the rhythmic ticking of a clock on the wall above,

Momoko broke the ice first, offering Hiro a cup of tea, hoping it would help alleviate some of the tension in the air. "Thanks," he nodded gratefully, accepting the offered drink. As he sipped the fragrant liquid, his eyes never left hers, studying every nuanced movement and expression intimately. "So, you wanted to talk?" he prompted cautiously, choosing his words carefully.

Swallowing a lump in her throat, Momoko leaned forward in her seat, struggling to find the appropriate words to begin recounting her tale. Eventually, she simply started talking without preface or introduction, her voice quivering slightly as she relayed events. "I'm sorry if this sounds crazy," she apologized, biting her lower lip. But Hiro merely shook his head, assuring her earnestly, "No need to apologize." His tender smile radiated compassion and acceptance, giving her the encouragement she needed to continue.

She recount every event, experience, and emotion she had undergone since her transformation into Momoko. She spoke about her previous existence as Yuki, describing how she used to live a normal life before the fateful encounter with the strange, magical voices. It was then when she had been granted a wish, an opportunity she seized upon without fully understanding the consequences. Little did she know that by asking for something so extraordinary, she would be thrust into a completely different reality, one where she would have to adapt to a new identity - Momoko. The process of adjusting to her new persona brought forth feelings of alienation and confusion, accompanied by unfamiliar desires emerging within her psyche. These transformations were not solely physical; her perspective on life also shifted drastically. Where once she viewed love and romantic pursuits from a distance, now she found herself yearning for affection. This dichotomy further exacerbated her

internal struggle,leading her deeper into conflict between the old self and the present. However, despite her initial unease regarding the transformation, a unique bond formed between Hiro and Momoko throughout their shared journey. Following the recounting of her vivid dream from the previous night, wherein she had felt as though she had somehow misplaced an integral aspect of her former self, Momoko at long last reached the end of her tale. She sat back, exhausted yet fulfilled by having shared such intimate details about herself with Hiro. Gently placing her teacup down onto the table beside her, she looked up to meet his solemn gaze, silently imploring him to understand and accept her.

Without saying anything, Hiro rose from his chair, walking slowly toward Momoko. Seeing her vulnerable state, Hiro couldn't resist reaching out to comfort her. Reaching out his hand towards her, he softly brushed away a loose strand of hair falling near her eye. "Momoko," he murmured tenderly, his voice barely more than a whisper. Feeling his touch against her cheek, she closed her eyes momentarily, absorbing the sensation. "You heard everything I said?" she questioned quietly, her voice trembling ever so slightly. Hiro nodded in confirmation, maintaining eye contact. "Yes, I listened closely." There was an extended pause. Finally, Momoko summoned enough courage to ask, "What do you think about my story?" Hiro considered his answer thoughtfully, searching for the most appropriate response amidst the complexity of his own conflicting emotions. In the depths of his heart, there lay undeniably strong affinity towards Momoko, evoking both concern and fascination. Yet, at the same time, he struggled to reconcile her dual nature, torn between understanding and bewilderment. Ultimately, he decided to communicate honestly and sincerely, expressing genuine care and sympathy for her predicament. As his fingers gently caressed her silky locks, gazing deeply into her eyes like the delicate petals of a cherry blossom tree, he spoke: "It might sound like a fantasy, but I promise you, I will always stand by your side no matter what happens". His reassurance provided solace for Momoko's troubled soul, easing her burden just a little. Nodding slightly, she gathered the courage to share her innermost fears. "I don't want to lose myself... or who I am now," confided Momoko. "Each day feels like I'm losing a piece of myself, slipping away into someone else entirely. And yet, the idea of returning to my old life seems increasingly distant and foreign..." Momoko confessed, letting her guard down gradually as she poured her heart out to Hiro. She described the internal battle she faced, oscillating between embracing her newfound passions and grappling with remnants of her past life. While the notion of returning to her original form held appeal due to familiarity, the prospect seemed daunting given her evolving perceptions of love and desire, it meant leaving behind everything she had grown to cherish in the world of Waku Waku Romance. Moreover, there existed the possibility that her true self might vanish forever into obscurity. Regardless, Momoko could not deny the thrill coursing through her veins whenever she interacted with Hiro. Though it pained her to acknowledge, she realized she had become captivated by him. Even while discussing grave matters, Hiro managed to instill a sense of calm and reassurance that Momoko hadn't encountered previously.

With his supportive demeanor, he helped ease her anxiety about merging two separate lives. Gradually, they moved closer together until their bodies touched. Desperate to feel connected again after so much turmoil, Momoko sought refuge in Hiro's arms, melting into his embrace like soft marshmallows. They remained close, nestled amongst the pillowy clouds of her plush mattress.

As time continued to tick away, her initial anxiety gradually faded into oblivion, giving way to an intense sensation that started at the pit of her stomach and spread outward like wildfire. The warmth coursing through her veins seemed to be emanating from deep within her body, surging upwards towards her chest and face, leaving her feeling flushed.As she pressed herself against Hiro, her lips parted slightly, inviting his gentle kisses which traveled across her cheeks, nose, and eventually onto her lips. Their tongues danced playfully against each other, a harmonious symphony of moans echoing in the silent chamber. Breathlessly, they pulled apart, catching their breath in unison. Looking into each other's eyes, their expressions conveyed a mutual longing.

Hiro lightly grasped Momoko's waist, pulling her closer, and she eagerly responded. Almost instinctively, their hands began roaming, exploring curves and contours, their hands sliding beneath each other's clothing, seeking warmth and stimulation.With an almost reverent slowness, they removed each layer, casting aside their clothes like ceremonial garments. Tenderly, they bared themselves to each other, taking pleasure in the sight of each other's forms.

As they stood face-to-face, their gazes met, locking onto one another, as their pupils dilated, reflecting the mounting desire within both of them. For Momoko, the thrill of being so close to him sent waves of excitement coursing through her body, causing her nerves to quiver and tremble with anticipation. Her heart raced, pounding against her chest, while her breath quickened, leaving her lightheaded. On the other side,

Hiro felt his own blood rushing through his veins, fueling his passionate urge for her. His penis was hard and insistent, seemingly alive with its own desires, craving touch and release. As he moved closer to her, his fingers traced the contours of her figure, exploring every curve and dip, sending delicious sensations through her entire frame.

With a gentle touch, his fingertips glided along the soft skin of her inner thighs, making her shiver involuntarily. Unable to contain her growing arousal anymore, Momoko guided Hiro's hand to cup her breast, allowing him to savor the fullness of her soft flesh through his palms. Overwhelmed by the heat and pressure building up between her legs, she squeezed Hiro's erection, delighting in the firm, pulsing weight within her grip.

The sensation of his manhood throbbing under her tightening grip ignited an even stronger longing within her, intensifying her hunger for satisfaction.

Grasping his shoulders, Momoko pushed Hiro onto the bed, positioning herself above him. With fierce determination, she lowered herself onto his member, taking him inside her welcoming folds. As she impaled herself upon him, her body shuddered with immense pleasure.

Moans escaped her lips, accompanied by ecstatic gasps as the tip of his penetrated her depths.She could feel every centimeter of his hardness pressing against her softness, sending waves of delightful sensations rippling throughout her entire frame.

Her hips rocked rhythmically, drawing him deeper into her core. The force of his thrusts intensified, creating a tantalizing friction against her sensitive flesh. Each powerful movement elicited a fresh wave of euphoria, flooding her system with pleasurable endorphins. Moans spilled forth from her lips, escaping in tandem with his groans. Her hands found purchase on either side of his shoulders, holding onto him tightly as she matched his fervent pace.

Every thrust brought an exquisite frisson of pleasure that radiated throughout her entire body. Her breath came faster, matching the intensity of their union.

Gripping the soft, cool fabric of the bed linens tightly, Momoko leaned forward, allowing herself to sink deeper into the embrace offered by Hiro. Her delicate frame nestled comfortably against him, as she buried her face into the crook of his neck, her sweet scent melding seamlessly with his masculine fragrance. Her ample breasts were nestled snugly against his torso, providing a natural cushion of feminine softness. As she pressed herself closer to him, the contours of her breasts became even more pronounced against his body, her nipples peaking with desire.

Closing her eyes, she savored the moment, relishing in the tender embrace that surrounded her, feeling completely secure in his loving arms. She moved her body rhythmically, her hips gently swaying back and forth as she continued to guide him deeper inside her warm, wet pussy. The sensation of having him fill her, stretching her flesh, was unlike anything she had ever experienced before. It made her feel complete, whole - something she had been missing since stepping foot into the world of Waku Waku Romance. She wanted nothing more than to remain wrapped around him eternally, absorbing every last drop of his essence. But all too soon, her body ached with pleasure and demanded relief. Her muscles contracted violently, signaling the beginning of her orgasm.

Each cell within her body trembled uncontrollably, resonating with an echo that reverberated through every pore of her skin. This palpable sensation was mirrored in Hiro as well, feeling her walls engulfing him, his cock twitched once then twice before finally erupting inside her. Throbbing deeply within her, his seed filled her womb. Her labia closed around him, milking him dry, coaxing him to release more seed. Spurts of semen shot from his rigid organ, filling her to capacity. Momoko held onto him even tighter, allowing herself to be consumed by the powerful explosion of his climax.

With every throb of his member, she felt his hot cum spewing into her depths, painting her insides with his salty liquid. Her own orgasm followed suit, sending shivers of bliss cascading throughout her entire frame. Feeling his hot semen oozing out of her depths, she couldn't help but let out a series of low, rapturous moans. The undulating waves of ecstasy crashed over her like the ocean, drowning her in sensory euphoria.

As her limbs went weak, she collapsed onto Hiro's chest, her sweaty body sticking to his bare skin. She felt his arms wrap protectively around her, holding her close. Their hearts still racing, Momoko and Hiro lay entwined amidst rumpled bedding, exhausted yet satisfied. Sweat dripped down their brows, trickling onto the soft fabric that caressed their tired frames. Momoko rested her head on Hiro's shoulder, whispering tender words of gratitude, her voice husky with satisfaction. Hiro tenderly ran his fingers through her silky locks, gently caressing her scalp as he moved downwards, stopping briefly to trace the curve of her earlobe with his thumb. She smiled contentedly, feeling cherished. Closing her eyes, she leaned into him, enjoying the warmth of his touch. Hiro shifted positions, placing himself behind her, running his fingers down her spine until reaching the small of her back. The featherlight brush of his fingertips caused goosebumps to rise on her skin, making her shiver with delight. Turning her head to face him, she locked eyes with him, smiling gently, her cheeks reddening. "Thank you," she murmured. Hiro simply nodded, returning her smile. Nuzzling into her hair, he inhaled her unique scent, a mix of peach, yuzu and subtle hints of her femininity that permeated his nostrils, making him want to bury his face there forever.

He loved how smooth her hair was – no split ends or knots marred its silkiness. Its rich pink color reminded him of sakura flower petals, falling gracefully during springtime. As he ran his fingers through it, she giggled, finding his playful affection endearing. Embracing her petite form closely, hisarms encircled her soft frame effortlessly, her rounded bottom fitting perfectly against his stomach.

They spent hours just talking about their lives, interests, hopes, dreams – ordinary things but significant for two people who have recently developed deep feelings for each other. In those quiet moments, Momoko shared stories of her time outside the digital realm; Hiro listened intently, occasionally offering his perspective and understanding. Both acknowledged that despite being born in different universes, their experiences weren't entirely dissimilar. There was a certain melancholy in realizing that their bond transcended virtual barriers, heightening the sense of isolation from reality. Hiro took Momoko's hand in his, intertwining their fingers together as they spoke about their respective journeys thus far. Momoko narrated tales of her struggle adapting to her newfound role within the game, the pressures she faced from her classmates and how much of her old self she lost after crossing over.

The sky began to darken, casting a warm golden glow cross their naked forms tangled in the sheets. Momoko nestled further into Hiro's embrace, appreciating the comfort he provided her, both physically and mentally. They lay silent for a while, taking in each other's presence, reveling in the solace they derived from one another. Hiro's hand idly played with strands of her hair, causing her to hum with enjoyment. His gentle caresses soothed her soul, easing away anxieties that lingered in the corners of her mind.

The soft sound of Momoko's stomach grumbling caught Hiro's attention. Realizing that they hadn't eaten dinner, he suggested ordering some food from nearby restaurants. Momoko eagerly agreed, excited to explore local cuisines available in the digital realm. She picked up her phone and quickly navigated through several menus, searching for something appetizing. Meanwhile, Hiro decided to take a quick shower, needing to freshen up after their passionate encounter.

Momoko couldn't help but observe him, admiring his lithe figure as he walked towards the bathroom. She noted the way his firm ass flexed as he disappeared beyond the door-frame. She quickly order some local favorites such as tempura, udon, and green tea ice cream. After confirming the delivery details, she decide to join Hiro in the bathroom. As steam billowed from under the door, she knocked lightly and entered, closing the door behind her. Stepping into the foggy space, she saw Hiro standing beneath the showerhead, water streaming down his body. The sight ignited a fire in her belly, stirring a different kind of hunger within her. With determination, she approached him slowly, letting her eyes rove hungrily across his wet, gleaming form. She reached out hesitantly, tracing a finger along the valley of his back, teasingly dipping lower, following the path of a tributary stream.

As Hiro playfully aimed the powerful spray of the showerhead towards her, he couldn't help but notice how entranced she appeared by the cascading stream of water. The chilly temperature of the water seemed to invigorate her as well, causing goosebumps to rise on her smooth skin. Despite being caught off guard by his impromptu move, she found herself unable to resist the refreshing impact of the water. With an unmistakable blush creeping across her cheeks, she took a step backward, instinctively moving out of the direct path of the pulsating jet. However, instead of retreating further, she chose to remain within the vicinity of the shower, allowing the glistening droplets to dance upon her body. As they struck her soft flesh, she reveled in the rejuvenating sensation that washed over her, feeling more alive than ever before. "Let's wash each other", Hiro proposed mischievously, raising a spark of excitement within Momoko. Excitement turned into anticipation as she nodded, agreeing to his suggestion. She stepped closer to him, feeling the heat radiating from his frame, mixed with the coolness of the mist lingering in the air. Water droplets clung to her voluminous locks, giving them a delicate sheen.

Hiro carefully scrubbed her long hair using her fragrant, yuzu soap. Watching her closely, he noticed the slight flush on her cheeks, attributing it to the warm shower and not embarrassment. He rinsed off, ensuring her hairs were cleaned thoroughly, before turning his attention to the other parts of her body. Using a gentle hands, he worked his way down, focusing particularly on her breasts - her prominent assets. Each breast responded differently, the left slightly firmer due to the pressure applied earlier while she had been lying beside him. The right, however, displayed clear signs of arousal, swollen with blood and achingly sensitive. This became evident as she squirmed nervously in his grasp, her breath hitching slightly. Her nipples hardened even more as his thumb circled them gently, eliciting involuntary gasps from her. He cupped her right breast fully, pinching the tip of her erect nipple between his index and middle fingers. The sudden surge of pleasure coursing through her veins caused her legs to quiver, leaving her momentarily weak in his embrace. Desire intensified in the depths of her core, urging her to reciprocate. Grabbing a handful of soap, she placed her palm flat against his chest, then slid it down along his torso, Her touch was light yet purposeful, slowly guiding her way downwards, ever so close to the object of her desire. Almost trembling with anticipation, she glided her slippery fingers around his penis, careful not to apply too much force which might cause him pain. Her touch was tentative, like that of a curious child exploring a forbidden treasure trove. She felt the pulse throbbing beneath her fingers, rhythmically vibrating with excitement. Her own heart raced, mirroring his steady beat. Feeling emboldened by their mutual connection, Momoko seized control, confidently applying a little pressure with her nimble fingers. She could feel his cock growing harder and longer beneath her touch, straining against her grip.

They continue to explore each other's bodies with tender care, losing themselves in the eroticism of their interactions. Their movements now synchronized, flowing seamlessly into one another, creating a symphony of moans and whimpers.

As Hiro continued to tenderly knead and caress Momoko's breasts, . With each gentle glide of her fingertips, she could hear him suck in sharp breaths, his entire body tensing with delight. His left hand squeezed her breast gently, rolling the nipple between his fingers as his other hand pulled her tightly against him. The smell of soap filled the air. Its scent melded with the sweet fragrances drifting throughout the bathroom, forming a heady mixture. It seemed almost fitting—the contrast of pure essences combining to create a unique atmosphere surrounding them. Closing his eyes, Hiro allowed himself to lose himself in the stimulating sensations assaulting his senses. Tenderly holding onto Momoko, he savored every tantalizing nuance of her body. As he held her securely, he relished in the silky texture of her hair. He marveled at the curve of her back, the perfect contours of her hips. The undeniably feminine softness of her body mesmerized him, filling him with an irresistible yearning. He could see the unbridled desire etched clearly on her face, illuminated by the warm light of the shower. Her cheeks flushed crimson, reflecting the intensity of their shared desires. She continue to gently caressed his erect phallus using her delicate fingertips, feeling the sturdy length pulsate rhythmically beneath her touch. Her heart raced faster as his member grew harder and longer. Unable to contain her curiosity, she moved her hand back toward her own wet folds, exploring her body. Hiro watched her intently, loving the open display of her womanhood. It made his manhood throb wildly, craving her touch. Gaze never breaking contact, she brought her hand back to his shaft, stroking it gently. Her movements were deliberately slow, accentuating the rising tension between them. With each pass of her hand, she increased the pace, pressing deeper and circling more rapidly. She knew exactly what buttons to press to drive him mad. Every thrust of her hand sent waves of pleasure shooting through his body, causing his muscles to twitch and convulse in ecstasy. He buried his lips in her neck, biting softly at her supple skin as his free hand began massaging her rounded bottom, digging deep into her curves with possessiveness.

The hot jets of water poured down upon them, washing away their accumulated sweat and lather. Amidst the chaos of falling liquid, their minds remained focused solely on each other. As if dancing to a silent melody, their bodies harmoniously aligned in syncopated movement.

As the shower's water splashed all around them, Momoko felt a sense of powerlessness beginning to take hold. Her body was becoming increasingly aware of its boundaries, begging for release. She arched her back as Hiro moved his hands expertly, taking charge of the situation. Moan after moan punctuated the ambient soundscape, merging with the pounding rhythms of the shower's waters. Increasing tempo and volume, her gasps escalated until reaching fever pitch as Hiro grazed her most sensitive spot. Both experienced the first brink of orgasm, drawing them closer together in their quest for fulfillment. In response, Momoko's fingers sped up their motion, working diligently to bring them both to climax. Hiro pushed forward, burying his mouth in her neck again, marking his territory as his tongue flickered against her soft skin.

The sound of the running water echoed in the confined space, creating a soothing backdrop to their steamy interlude. Hiro groaned deeply as he finally reached his peak. A surge of white-hot fluid shot forth from his engorged member, covering her pale flesh in streaks of ecstatic release. Momoko followed suit, joining him in the dizzying heights of pleasure. Her inner walls contracted rhythmically around his finger.

They stood there, still entwined under the showerhead, reveling in the afterglow of their passionate

encounter. They wrapped their arms around each other once more, drawing comfort from each other's presence.

Having found solace in each other's company, they gradually disengaged from one another, stepping apart respectfully. Standing side by side, they assessed one another, admiring their physical beauty. A playful smile crossed Momoko's features as she took note of how Hiro looked at her. The look in his eyes betrayed his appreciation for her form. Gaining confidence from his reaction, Momoko smiled demurely, running her fingers through her tousled hair. Hiro returned the gesture, capturing her expression in his memory.

Stepping out of the shower, they wrap themselves in warm towels. Hiro helps dry Momoko's curved figure, passing the cloth gently across her skin, occasionally stopping to give extra attention to her ample bosom. The soft fabric caresses her smooth shoulders, skimming gracefully over her defined collarbones.

After they had thoroughly dried themselves off with thick, warm towels, Hiro helped Momoko put on a fresh set of clothes. Delightedly, he noticed how well her garments complimented her voluptuous shape, highlighting her best features. She wore a short blue yukata with flowers painted along the hemline. Adorning her waist, a wide obi secured the ensemble, cinching the knot behind her back. The thin material clung to her slim frame, hinting at the curves concealed beneath. As always, her long hair fell loose down her back, framing her exquisite features perfectly.

Hiro couldn't help but notice the faint blush that colored her cheeks, a testament to their recent encounter. He felt a wave of tenderness towards her as he observed her reaction. It made him want nothing more than to protect and cherish her - the idea of her vulnerability stirring something primal within him. His eyes traced the lines of her petite nose before lingering on her full lips, inviting him further into their realm of hidden mysteries.

Suddenly, the doorbell rang, bringing them back to reality. Momoko quickly tied the obi around her waist, ensuring everything was neatly arranged.

Reaching the front door, Momoko peeked through the frosted glass panel beside the door before she opened it, greeting the delivery person with a friendly yet guarded demeanour. Tacking the package, she confirm its contents and delivery address. Once satisfied, she handed over payment for the service. After closing the door, Momoko turned to Hiro, leading him towards the kitchen, eager to partake in the meal that would sustain them during their night ahead.

Understanding her intentions, Hiro agreed without hesitation. As they sat down near the table, the anticipation hung heavy in the air. With careful precision, they served portions onto their respective plates, giving thanks. Their laughter filled the space, adding warmth to the cozy ambiance. Overcome with excitement, they devoured the succulent food ravenously, indulging in the various flavors, textures, and temperatures.

After finishing dinner, the couple decided to settle in for the evening. Momoko led Hiro to her bedroom, where the comfortable, ornamental decor invited relaxation. Embracing the moment, they settled into a tender embrace, slowly savoring each other's touches. Momoko nestled herself snugly against Hiro, his hardened member poking at her hip slightly. His hands roamed over her soft curves, leaving goosebumps in their wake. As Hiro tenderly unwrapped the delicate fabric that encircled Momoko's waist. He found himself unable to resist the allure of her unadulterated flesh as she gently removed her yukata, revealing an expanse of flawless skin that seemed to radiate warmth and invitation. Underneath, she donned only a stripped panties which accentuated her voluptuous derrière. Naked except for the thin piece of cloth clinging to her female attributes, she displayed her beautiful physique. With her rosy nipples perked upward, arousing his curiosity, Hiro wanted nothing more than to taste those sweet buds. Her breasts swayed hypnotically as she moved, teasing him even more. She leaned in close, allowing him to catch whiffs of her scent. Hiro kissed her, slowly moving downwards, exploring every curve, hill, and valley of her body with his lips.

They lay on the soft mattress, surrounded by velvety pillows, breathing heavily, their hearts throbbing in tandem. Hiro pressed his face into her neck, letting his fingers explore the landscape of her naked body. He fondled her ripe breasts, eliciting a mixture of pain and desire from her. She writhed beneath him, urging him on. Meanwhile, his hands explored every crevice, finding new ways to stimulate her. Soft kisses and gentle whispers poured into her ears, setting her pulse racing.

As she lay beneath him, her body trembling with anticipation, she felt his strong hands grasping her hips, pulling her closer towards him. His fingers dug into her flesh, leaving an indelible mark that spoke volumes about his desire and determination. He moved towards her, slowly advancing, until the tip of his manhood glided sensually along her folds. Her breath quickened, her eyes locked with his, silently promising submission.

With calculated movements, he positioned himself at her entrance. As he penetrated her tight passage, they moaned in perfect synchronicity. Each stroke drove them deeper into the abyss of passion. His body shivered with delight, as hers quaked with need. She held his head to her chest, feeling the intensity build up inside her. She bit her lip, attempting to stifle her moans. He matched her fervor, thrusting harder while whispering endearments in her ear.

Momoko wrapped her legs around him, drawing him even closer, deepening their connection. Hiro shifted his pace, varying his angles and depth, seeking to hit her most sensitive areas just right. Every powerful stroke sent waves of pleasurable agony coursing through her core. He cupped her breast firmly, pinching her already swollen nipple gently, driving her wild with lust. Her moans grew ever louder, indicating her mounting satisfaction.

Hiro increased the tempo, matching her enthusiasm. Every powerful strike caused her body to convulse violently. With every movement, his raw masculinity rubbed against her intimately. She could feel his erection pressing against her sex, stroking her insides deliciously. Feeling incredibly turned on, Momoko instinctively began grinding her hips against him. Her moans echoed throughout the room, testifying to the intensity of their union.

In that moment, Hiro couldn't help but revel in the sight of Momoko losing herself to pleasure, he loved seeing her lose control, becoming increasingly desperate for release. Her soft, wet folds clenched around his length, milking him hungrily. Unable to contain his own building desire, Hiro released his seed into her, filling her completely. Emitting muffled sounds of ecstasy, Momoko welcomed the flood of his essence, her body absorbing it entirely. Spent, they lay together, embracing each other lovingly.

Hiro gazed affectionately at Momoko's sleeping visage, relishing the afterglow of their intense coupling. Her tousled hair cascaded across her pale skin like a waterfall of pink strands. The moonlight danced seductively upon her exposed skin, casting an ethereal glow across her curves. Clutching the sheet to his side, Hiro marveled at the beauty resting peacefully beside him. Reveling in the euphoria of their shared experience, they drifted towards a deep, rejuvenating sleep. Dreaming of their future together, their bodies entangled under the covers, comfortably nestling together.

LIVING AS MOMOKO

After countless years had passed since Yuki found himself awakening anew as Momoko, the two lovers were now able to enjoy a harmonious existence together as husband and wife. Both Hiro and Momoko lived out their days happily in love, creating memories filled with both joy and eroticism. As time went on, Momoko and Hiro continued to cultivate their relationship, exploring every possible aspect of their sexuality. In these moments, they found solace and freedom, immersing themselves fully in one another's arms.

Living together brought forth many joys – the simple act of sharing breakfast became more enjoyable as they laughed over stories from the previous day. . This strengthened bond enabled them to navigate complex issues that arose, tackling problems collaboratively. The daily tasks of household chores took on a renewed sense of purpose and meaning, knowing that these efforts contributed to their shared home life. Most importantly, they discovered endless possibilities of expressing their affections in unique ways.

During quiet evenings spent cuddling under soft blankets, they enjoyed exploring each other's minds through conversation. Sharing dreams, aspirations, fears, and secret desires allowed them to grow stronger as partners.

Their love blossomed into something beautiful, a child was born, their family expanded, and their lives evolved into a happy balance of responsibility and play. They navigated the highs and lows of married life gracefully, cherishing each other deeply. Intimacy remained essential, feeding the flames of their passion.

The child grew into a spirited young boy named Yuki, who quickly developed an interest in video games. Momoko. watched closely as his son eagerly conquered levels in the same virtual realms he once frequented. It sparked nostalgia and amusement, reminding her of how far she'd come since then.

65